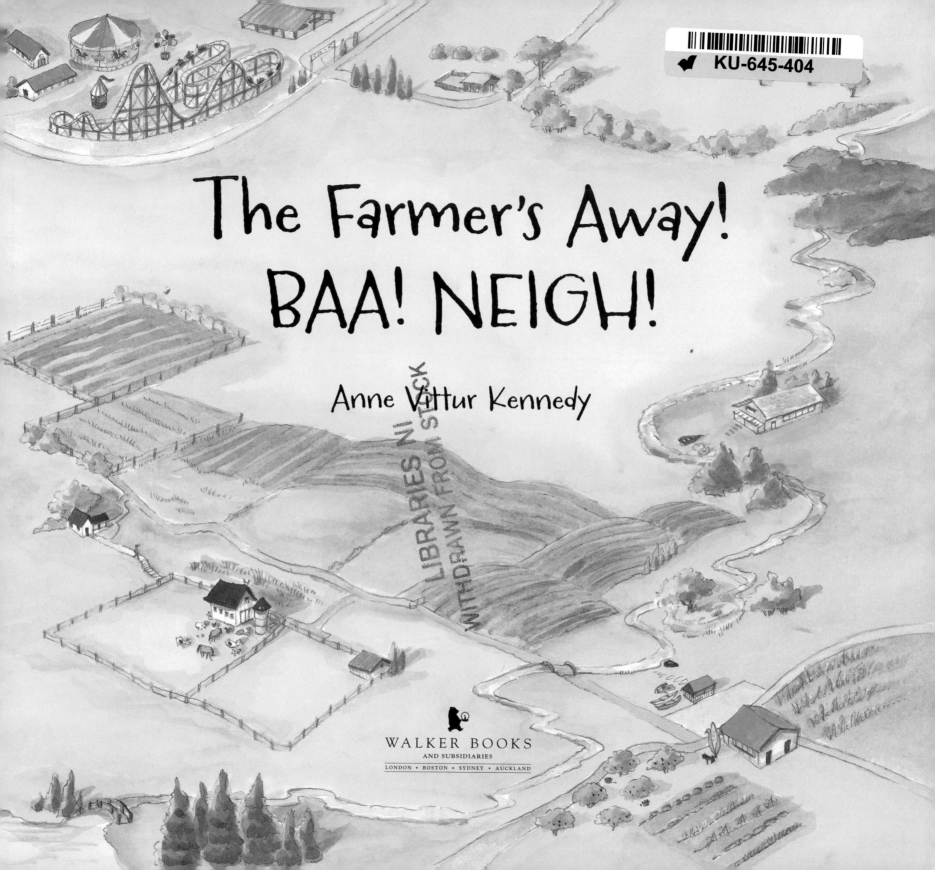

The Farmer's Away! BAA! NEIGH!

Anne Vittur Kennedy

WALKER BOOKS
AND SUBSIDIARIES

LONDON · BOSTON · SYDNEY · AUCKLAND

ribbet mama ribbet mama
eek honk quack

splish splash baa baa
moo moo yap

arf neigh cluck cluck
cock-a-doodle-doo

mama mew mama mew
splish neigh moo

sss sss sss sss
yap sss eek

bzz bzz bzz bzz
quack bzz tweet

cock-a-doodle-doo moo
ribbet ribbet sss

baa cheep baa cheep
oink oink bzz

hmm . . . hmm . . .

neigh arf neigh moo
mew mew mew

neigh neigh baa baa
moo moo tweet

honk honk oink oink
arf cheep eek

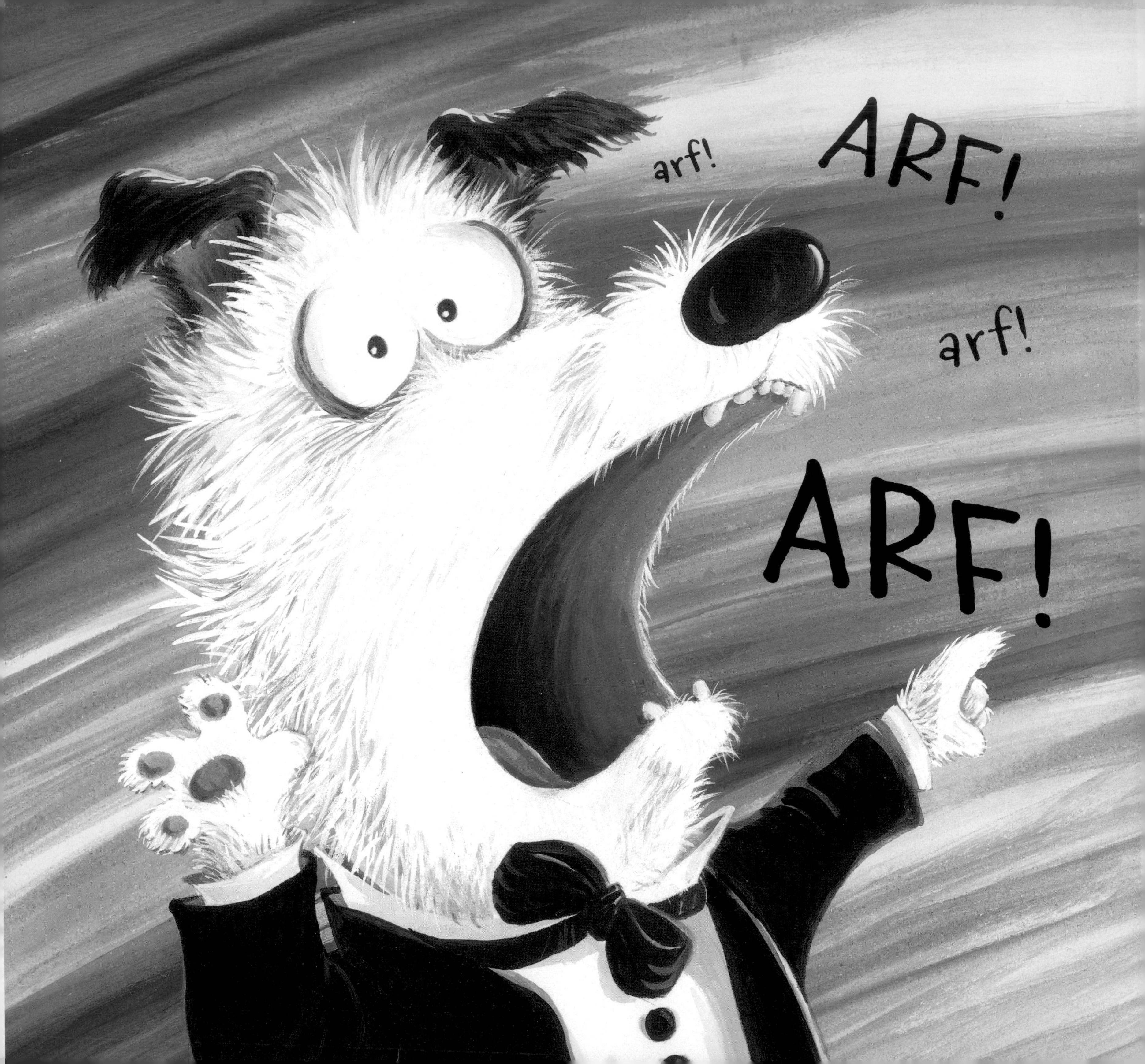
arf!
ARF!
arf!
ARF!

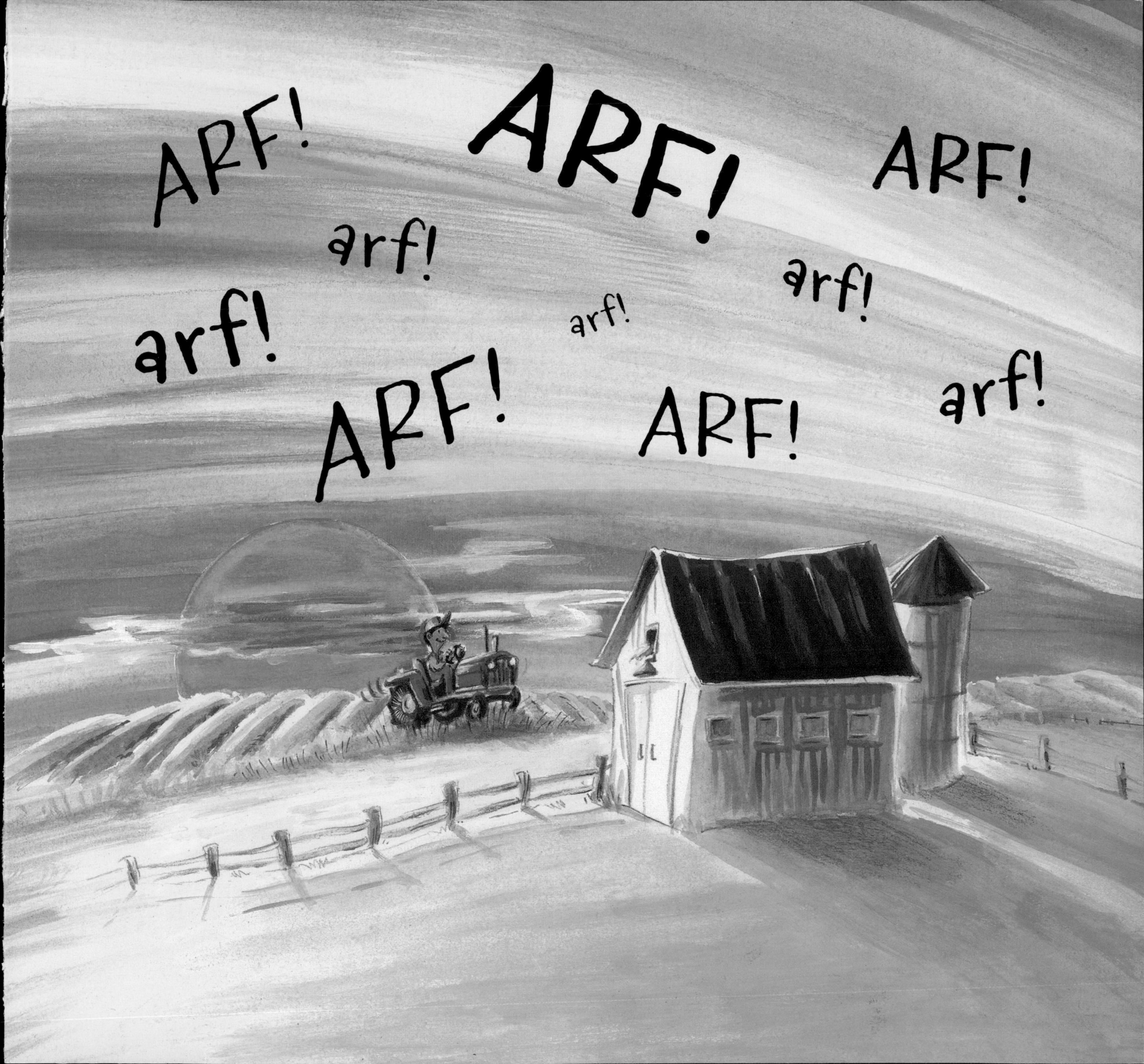
ARF!
ARF!
ARF!
arf!
arf!
arf!
arf!
arf!
ARF!
ARF!

shh shh shh shh
shh shh shhhhhhhh

shh shh shh shh
shh shh shhhhhhhh

arf

yap

neigh

baa

mew

quack

cluck

mama

moo

splish

splash

honk

tweet

cheep